Mokele-mbembe

Jan E. Culbertson

Mokele-mbembe

Copyright © 2014 by Jan E. Culbertson

Dedication

This book is dedicated to all my grandchildren: Bianca; Alyssa; Austin; Alani; Stephanie; Sienna; and Leo. They have all brought so much joy into my life, but also encouraged me to write this book.

INTRODUCTION

Since the beginning of time man has told stories and legends of strange creatures and monsters. These stories and legends are not unique to any one country or continent, they are universal throughout the world.

But sometimes animals that were thought to be either folklore legends or extinct are discovered. The Mountain Gorilla was thought to be a myth until 1847, and the Okapi, a half zebra half antelope-like mammal was discovered within the last hundred years. Also the Coelacanth, a prehistoric fish, was thought to be extinct until 1938 when a woman caught one off the coast of Africa.

In the United States we have Bigfoot; in Mexico they have the Chupacabra; in Canada the Ogopogo; in Tibet they have the Yeti; and in the West Indies the Loogaroo. In the Congo they have the Mokele-mbembe, a large dinosaur-like animal that inhabits the Congo River.

This is the fictional story of an expedition that hopes to either capture or kill the Mokele-mbembe. Capturing or killing any large wild animal is dangerous but when the animal is a throwback to the Mesozoic Period, it is not only dangerous, it is insane!

CHAPTER ONE

For the past two years thirty seven year old Dr. Marsha Styles had had been on digs in the Gobi Desert in western China looking for fossilized eggs of various dinosaur species. The Chinese government had invited Marsha on the expedition because she had advanced degrees in biology, zoology, and paleontology, and was considered to be a leading expert on fossilized dinosaurs and their eggs.

Now the expedition was completed, and in the morning a government helicopter would arrive and fly her to Chengdu. From Chengdu she would catch a plane to Beijing and from there another flight back to the United States. Within a week she would be back in her apartment in San Francisco.

Back in her tent she sat on her cot thinking about all they had accomplished during the past two years. They had discovered several raptor nests full of fossilized eggs, and also bones of many small bird-sized dinosaurs that still had to be analyzed to determine exactly what species they belonged to. She had photographs of everything they found stored in her laptop and she planned on writing a book about the expedition when she got home.

She opened her laptop to add the photographs from that day. As she was plugging her camera into the computer she noticed that she had an email from her friend Bruce Millard.

She and Bruce had gone to school together and had kept in touch off and on ever since. While in school they had dated a few times but they became such good friends that it seemed weird to kiss each other, much less have sex, so they stopped dating.

She enjoyed his friendship even if he was sort of a wild man when it came to paleontology. He had this crazy theory that somewhere in the world at least one species of dinosaur must have survived the mass extinction. Nobody took him seriously except some crypto zoologists that thought the same thing.

Marsha opened the email and read it. *"Marsha, I heard you were in China, but I hope you are free now to come to Africa. I know you think I'm crazy, but I believe I have actual physical evidence of a group of water animals resembling Plesiosaurs living in the Congo River and its tributaries. The locals call the animal Mokele-mbembe. I beg you to come and promise you will not be disappointed. Will be waiting for you in the Venus Hotel in Kinshasha. Best regards, Bruce."*

She read the email over and over again. The words "actual physical evidence" popped out at her. Bruce was a crazy bastard, but he wasn't a liar. If he believed he had evidence of a plesiosaur type animal that was strong enough to bother her half way around the world, he must have something pretty substantial.

Even if what he had wasn't all that great, a trip on the Congo River would be a nice change after being stuck in the Gobi Desert for two years. Besides she had always wanted to see the Congo River after reading Joseph Conrad's ***"Heart of Darkness"*** in college. Her answer to his email was short and sweet. *"Bruce, what room are you in?"*

Marsha loaded the new photos into her laptop and turned it off. Just then a voice said "Knock, knock," and Dr. Chang opened the flap of her tent and stuck his head in. "Good evening Dr. Chang, what's up?" she asked.

"Well, tonight is the last night you will be with us, so we have planned a little 'Goodbye' dinner for you. Would you be so kind as to come to the dining tent with me?" he asked.

Dr. Chang was the scientist in charge of the expedition and he was a wonderful man about sixty years old. He had done everything within his power to ensure that Marsh and the other women on the expedition had everything they needed. He had even had ice cream flown in every week, and made sure there were plenty of English speaking movies on DVDs, and even popcorn.

She took Chang's hand and he led her to the dining tent. While they were walking he told her how much he appreciated her contribution to the expedition, and how he was going to miss her.

As they entered the tent Marsha saw that the entire expedition team was there. On the far end of the tent they had hung a large banner reading, "Farewell Marsha," and everybody broke out singing what she guessed was the Chinese version of "For she's a jolly good fellow!"

Dr. Chang had somehow performed another miracle and arranged to have cold champagne and oysters on the half shell among the many other delicious treats for Marsha's going away dinner. Half way through the dinner Dr. Chang got up and made a speech about how much the entire crew enjoyed working with Marsha and how much her expertise contributed to the success of the expedition. Dr. Chang was followed by other members of the team, each one recounting anecdotal information about how Marsha had helped them.

When the Chinese had all finished their speeches Dr. Chang called Marsha up to where he was standing, and presented her with a gold wristwatch. On the back was inscribed, *"To Dr. Styles, a good friend and great scientist."*

Marsha felt compelled to make a short thank you speech. She thanked everyone for being so nice to her during the past year, and for accepting her as part of their team. She assured them that she would never forget them, and that if she ever had the opportunity to return to China on another expedition, she would accept in a heartbeat.

The rest of the evening was a blur of people hugging her, drinking glass after glass of champagne, and eating way too much rich food. When the party broke up at about two in the morning Marsha was feeling decidedly tipsy. She returned to her tent and flopped down on her cot with her clothes on and immediately fell asleep.

When she awoke in the morning her head was throbbing like crazy. She should have known better than to drink so much champagne, but she got caught up in the moment and overindulged.

Marsha swung her legs over the side of the cot and stood up. Big mistake! Before her head was just throbbing with a dull pain, now it felt like she had an entire band of bass drums beating wildly inside her head. She walked to the first aid tent and got some aspirin for the pain. Then she went to the dining tent and got a cup of coffee and two eggs over easy.

She wolfed down the eggs as fast as she could because she had to shower, change clothes, and pack. She looked at her new watch. It was a little after nine and the helicopter was supposed to come for her at eleven o'clock. As she headed for the showers she wished she could go back to sleep for a few more hours.

Somehow Marsha managed to be ready when the helicopter landed to fly her to Chengdu. It was one of those big military helicopters that could carry about twenty passengers. As the big machine neared the ground to land the rotors threw up large clouds of fine red Gobi dust.

When the dust settled, the men of the expedition began unloading the supplies the helicopter had brought. In less than half an hour it was emptied and refueled and ready to takeoff.

While she was waiting to board the aircraft, Dr. Chang came up and gave her a hug and thanked her once again for all her help during the expedition. She started to grab her two suitcases but Chang picked them up and carried them to the helicopter for her.

One of the helicopter crewmen helped her get strapped into the canvas bottomed seat, He also tied down her two suitcases so they wouldn't rattle around inside the aircraft.

Marsha listened as the pilot revved up the helicopter's engines and the rotor blades began turning, slowly at first then faster and faster. Suddenly the aircraft leapt into the air and ascended at a nose-down angle.

She wished the helicopter had a window so she could watch the landscape below as they flew over it. The aircraft flew in a large circle all the while gaining altitude and then leveled off and headed for Chengdu. It was a flight of several hours and despite the loud roar of the engines and the uncomfortable canvas seat Marsha managed to fall asleep.

When the helicopter's landing gear bumped down on the tarmac at Chengdu she awoke with a start. She had been in such a deep sleep that it took her a couple seconds to realize where she was.

The aircraft taxied over to one of the passenger loading pads and the pilot shut off the engine. As soon as the rotor blades slowed down enough one of the ground crew opened the helo's door and extended a short ladder for the passengers to exit the aircraft.

Marsha got out of the helicopter and one of the crewmen handed her bags to her. She walked into the airport terminal and looked around for the Air China ticket counter. She already had her ticket from Chengdu to Beijing, but now needed to exchange it for a ticket to Mumbai, India if possible.

As Marsha walked up to the Air China ticket counter she prepared herself for the grueling ordeal of making herself understood by the Chinese girl at the counter. Much to her surprise the girl spoke perfect English with just a slight trace of an accent. More importantly, she understood exactly what Marsha wanted to do and within a few minutes she had exchanged Marsha's Beijing ticket for one to Mumbai. Of course there was an additional charge of 2,681.00 yuan. As Marsha pulled out her Visa card and handed it to her, the girl said, "That comes to $440.00 in American dollars."

As the girl was making out her ticket and boarding pass Marsha asked, "Miss, can you tell me how long the flight is from here to Mumbai, India?"

The girl punched some keys on her computer and said, "The flight time from here to Mumbai, India is five hours." As she handed Marsha her ticket, boarding pass, and baggage claim ticket she said, "Your flight number is 941, and it departs from gate 7 in about two hours. Don't forget to go through immigration and customs before going to the boarding area."

"Okay, thank you very much," Marsha said. With two hours to kill before her flight left she decided to find a restaurant and get some lunch. "Where are the restaurants located?" she asked the girl at the counter.

"There is a large food court just down that way," she replied pointing the direction.

"Thanks again for all your help," Marsha said.

After a short walk Marsha spotted the food court up ahead. As she drew closer to it she couldn't believe her eyes. There, in the airport terminal in Chengdu, China, was a Kentucky Fried Chicken and a McDonald's restaurant! She went up to the counter at McDonald's and ordered a Big Mac, French fries, and a coke.

Although she knew that nutrition experts were saying that fast food was bad for one's health, she savored each and every bite of her hamburger. After a diet consisting almost entirely of Chinese food for the last two years, an American hamburger seemed like a real delicacy.

When she finished eating Marsha went to the immigration and customs area. The officials there checked her passport and approved her exit from the country. Then she went to the Gate 7 waiting area and took a seat. She wished she had a book or magazine to read to pass the time until they called her flight. Then she began thinking about her friend Bruce, and wondering what kind of evidence he might have that there were plesiosaur-like animals living in the Congo River.

At last her flight was called and she got in line to show her boarding pass and ticket and board the plane. Most of the other passengers were Indians, and a few of the women were dressed in colorful saris. She made a mental note to buy one if she had a chance while in Mumbai. They looked very comfortable and besides a nice colorful sari would make a good souvenir.

She took her seat between two Indian women who although they smiled at her didn't seem overly friendly. That was fine with Marsha because she didn't feel much like talking anyway.

As soon as they were airborne the flight attendant came and took her order for a Scotch and soda. She was still a little shaky from drinking so much champagne the night before and figured a little hair of the dog that bit her might make her feel better.

Three Scotch and sodas later she was feeling a lot better when they landed in Mumbai! After leaving the plane and collecting her baggage she began looking for an airline that had a flight to Kenshasha, Congo, sometime soon.

It appeared that Kenya Airways had the first flight leaving for Nairobi and then on to Kinshasha, but it wasn't departing until tomorrow morning at ten o'clock. She made her reservation for that flight and was given her ticket and boarding pass. She asked the ticket clerk if she could recommend a good hotel close to the airport here in Mumbai, and the girl recommended Hotel Sahara Star. According to her it was a very nice hotel only a few minutes away.

Marsha grabbed a taxi and had the driver take her to the Hotel Sahara Star. The ticket counter girl was right, it was a nice hotel. She booked a room for the night, and after putting her bags in her room she took a quick shower and headed down to the hotel restaurant.

It had been a long time since Marsha had eaten Indian food, so she ordered Biryani and Tandoori chicken. A bottle of cold Kingfisher beer was her choice of drink while she waited for her food to be served. She set aside the glass the waiter brought her and took a sip directly from the bottle. The taste surprised her. She had grown accustomed to the rather bitter taste of Tsingtao beer while in China, and the full hearty flavor of the Kingfisher was a welcome change.

After finishing her dinner Marsha walked through the large hotel lobby doing some window shopping at the many shops located there. She went inside one of the shops that had several saris in the display window. When she walked out of the little shop she was carrying a bag with two beautiful silk saris inside.

Back in her room Marsha watched television for a while and then went to sleep. She didn't want to be sleepy when she boarded the plane in the morning.

She awoke the following morning at seven o'clock, showered, got dressed, and went down to the hotel dining room for some breakfast. Two eggs over easy, some hash brown potatoes, and a cup of hot coffee later Marsha was ready to face whatever lay ahead that day.

Back to her room, a packing of her suitcases, and a quick taxicab ride to the airport and Marsha was ready to board the Kenya Airways flight to Kinshasha. She was lucky enough to get a window seat on the plane, so when they took off and headed out over the Indian Ocean she had a good view of the topaz blue carpet below.

Occasionally, that beautiful blue expanse of ocean was marred by a merchant ship scurrying across it carrying cargo to some port or other. Within an hour Marsha grew weary of watching the never ending blue and dozed off.

The loud screech of the landing gear as it first touched down on the runway awakened Marsha. She looked out the window and saw it was a bright sunny day in Nairobi.

She had been in Nairobi once several years ago when she was on her way to a dig in the Olduvai Gorge in Tanzania. On that occasion, just as this one, she didn't leave the airport, so she really had no idea what the city was like.

The flight attendant announced that those passengers continuing on to Kinshasha would have a layover of approximate one hour while the aircraft was being serviced. All the passengers exited the airplane and Marsha went inside the terminal to find a place where she might get a sandwich.

It didn't take long to find a place where she could get a toasted ham and cheese sandwich and a coke. As she sat there eating her sandwich her mind turned to what her friend Bruce had said in his email. She was intrigued by what he had said about having evidence of a group of water animals resembling plesiosaurs. Bruce was well aware of how she felt about crytpozoologists and their weird theories about strange monster-like animals living in isolation in different places throughout the world. Therefore, she knew that he wouldn't bring her half way around the world on a wild goose chase.

By the time she finished her sandwich and soda it was nearly time to board the plane again for the final leg of her journey to Kinshasha. She went to the boarding gate and waited for the flight to be called.

Soon she was on the plane again and they were airborne headed for the Congo. From her window Marsha had a good view of the vastness of the African continent, or at least the part they flew over. There were vast savannas with large herd of animals, and dense jungles where all one could see was the green tops of the trees and the occasional dark ribbon of a river.

Three and a half hours after taking off from Nairobi, Kenya, the plane was landing at Kinshasha, Republic of the Congo. As the plane was taxiing to one of the passenger loading gates the pilot came on the intercom and thanked everyone for flying with Kenya Airways.

As soon as the boarding tunnel be was connected the passengers began exiting the plane. Marsha was one of the last to leave. Inside the terminal she located the baggage claim area and after looking at what seemed like hundreds of pieces of luggage, she found her suitcases.

She grabbed a taxi in front of the terminal and told the driver to take her to the Venus Hotel. "Is Memsaab sure she wants to go to the Venus Hotel, the Sultani Hotel is much better," the driver told her. Marsha knew that taxi drivers in many countries get a commission if they take their passengers to the hotel they have a deal with.

"No, I want to go the Venus Hotel to meet a friend there," she told him.

CHAPTER TWO

When the taxi pulled up in front of the Venus Hotel she was surprised. She had imagined it to be some sort of dump, but it really wasn't that bad. She went to the front desk and after registering for a room she asked what room Bruce was in. "Mr. Millard is in room number 19, but he's not in his room right now," the desk clerk told her.

"I'm not going to my room right now, but could you please have someone take my bags to my room?" she asked.

"Yes, of course Memsaab," the clerk replied.

Marsh knew that if Bruce wasn't in his room he had to be in the bar, so that's where she headed. She was right. As soon as she walked in she saw him seated at the bar. She eased up behind him and put her hands over his eyes. "Guess who?" she said.

"Marsha!" he said loudly. "I'm so glad you could come, it's been way too long since we've seen each other," he said as he turned on the barstool and gave her a big hug.

"I know, I feel the same way. After school we each went our own way and we seldom get to see each other anymore," Marsha told him.

"Let me buy you a drink and we'll sit at a table and get caught up," Bruce suggested.

"A Scotch and soda sounds real good," she told him.

Bruce carried their drinks over to one of the tables and they sat down. Marsha took a sip of her drink and said, "Okay Bruce, tell me about this river monster you discovered."

He hesitated a moment. "Well, natives here in the Congo have a legend or myth, or whatever the hell you want to call it, of an animal they call Mokele-mbembe, he told her.

"What kind of animal is this Mokele-mbembe?" she asked.

"From everything I can gather from talking to many natives who say they have seen it, it sounds to me like a plesiosaur," Bruce replied.

"Come on Bruce, you know that plesiosaurs have been extinct for millions of years," Marsha reminded him.

"I didn't say it is a plesiosaur Marsha, I said it sounded like one to me. Just consider this. The Congo River is about 2,900 miles long, with depths of over 200 feet in many places. Also, the Congo has over 10,000 miles of tributary rivers feeding into it. Most of that almost 13,000 miles of rivers passes through uninhabited areas. Don't you think it might be possible that there is some large mammal or reptile living in those waters that hasn't been discovered yet?" he asked.

"Well, when you put it that way I guess there is a small chance that there is some undiscovered animal in the river. In your email you said something about having some kind of proof of such an animal, what is your evidence?" she asked.

"It's only circumstantial evidence, but to me it seems pretty convincing. I would rather show it to you than tell you what it is, but we have to go to Kisangani," he told her.

"Why didn't you just bring the evidence with you here to Kinshasha?" Marsha asked.

"The evidence is biological in nature and I have it stored in an ice house in Kisangani to keep it from deteriorating in this hot weather," he told her.

"Well, I came this far, so I guess I'll have to go to Kisangani with you. How are we going to get there?" she asked.

"Tomorrow morning I'll charter a small plane to fly us there. It's only a few hours from here," Bruce replied.

"Okay, now tell me what the hell you have been doing since we last saw each other," Marsha told him.

They spent the next two hours getting caught up on each other's lives and careers. Bruce told her that before coming to the Republic of the Congo and searching for the Mokelembembe he had been working in Croatia. He said they had discovered a treasure-trove of Neandertal artifacts in the Vindija cave there. "Before that I was an adjunct professor of paleontology for nearly two years at Berkeley, in California," he told her.

"Now that surprises me Bruce. I never took you for one to let himself be confined within the halls of academia," Marsh replied.

"Well, you're right about that. I was going nuts there," he said. "I know you've been in China, so tell me about it," he asked.

They spent the several hours talking about their lives and work, until finally it was time for dinner. They went to the hotel dining room and continued their conversation over dinner.

When they finished eating, Marsha invited Bruce up to her room so she could show him all the photos she had on her laptop. She knew he would be impressed by the many photos she had of dinosaur eggs in nests.

Bruce was indeed impressed by her photos and suggested she make them into a book about her experience on the expedition in the Gobi Desert. "That is exactly what I plan on doing," she told him.

Bruce looked at his watch, "Oh my God, it's late. We better get to bed so we can be up early tomorrow for our flight to Kisangani."

Marsha hadn't been with a man for the entire time she was in China and she desperately wanted to ask Bruce to spend the night with her, but instead she said, "Yeah, you're right. We better get to bed. Good night Bruce."

In the morning they met in the dining room for breakfast, and afterwards got their luggage and hailed a taxi. Bruce told the driver to take them to the N'Dolo Airport.

When Marsha heard that she asked, "Why aren't we going to the regular airport?"

"Our pilot Buck keeps his plane at N'Dolo," he replied.

"Oh, you've already chartered the plane then?" she asked.

"Well, sort of. Buck has been flying me around the Congo ever since I got here. He's a nice guy and best of all he is cheap, so I can afford him. I called him early this morning and told him we wanted to fly to Kisangani today," Bruce told her.

When they reached the airport Bruce directed the taxi driver to take them to a rundown hangar at the north end of the field. In front of the hangar was an old Beechcraft airplane that looked like a relic from World War Two.

They got out of the taxi and Bruce shouted, "Buck, we're here!"

An old man wiping grease from his hands with a rag came strolling out of the hangar. He was dressed in a blue denim shirt and was wearing overalls. "Good morning Bruce, looks like we have good flying weather this morning," the man said, looking up at the sky.

"Buck, this is my friend Marsha. She's going with us to Kisangani," Bruce said.

The man held out his hand to Marsha and said, "Glad to meet you Marsha, I'm Ray Buckley, but everybody just calls me Buck. Bruce told me he was bringing a woman with him this morning, but he didn't tell me you was so pretty."

Buck was close enough so that when he spoke Marsha could smell the alcohol on his breath. She shook his offered hand and said, "You are too kind. Glad to meet you too."

"You folks excuse me while I go in and wash up. You can go ahead and put your baggage in the plane and I'll be out in a flash and we can get going," he said.

As soon as the pilot was out of sight Marsha turned to Bruce and said, "You've got to be kidding Bruce, that guy has been drinking already this morning, and his plane looks like it belongs in the Smithsonian Museum!"

"Look, I know Buck drinks a little, but he is a very good pilot. He flew recon aircraft in the Vietnam War, and after the war he flew a news helicopter in Portland, Oregon for a few years. After that he was a bush pilot in Alaska for over twenty years, and now for about the last ten years he has been flying all over Africa," he told her.

"And it doesn't bother you that he has been drinking?" Marsha asked.

"He probably flies better when he's had a few drinks. Anyway, I've flown all over the Congo with him and I trust him completely," he replied.

"Bruce, you're a crazy bastard, and we'll probably crash in the jungle and be killed, but I'll go with you," Marsha said laughing.

They put their luggage in the back of the plane and waited for Buck to come out of the hangar. About ten minutes later he came out dressed in a clean but threadbare military olive drab flight suit. "Okay folks, let's get going," he said. Marsha was surprised that he now seemed to be completely sober.

Buck climbed into the cockpit and took his seat. "One of you can sit up here with me if you want," he told them.

Bruce looked at Marsha. "Why don't you go sit in the cockpit with Buck, that way you'll get a really good view of the vastness of this place," Bruce told her.

She would much rather be in the front where she had a good view than in the rear passenger section where there were only small windows that provided a limited view of the ground below. Marsha went up to the cockpit and took the left hand seat and put on her seat belt.

Buck started turning over the port engine first. The propeller began turning slowly at first and then it sounded as if something in the engine exploded, a large cloud of black smoke spewed out of the engine, and the propeller stopped turning.

"Come on baby, you can do it for Papa," Buck said, talking to the aircraft. He started turning the engine over again. This time after the same small explosion sound the propeller began turning faster and faster, and soon it became obvious that it wasn't going to stop again. Then he performed the same ritual with the starboard engine.

He taxied out to the end of the rustic runway and pushed the throttles forward revving up both engines. The plane began to shake violently, and Marsha was getting worried when Buck released the brakes and the plane suddenly lurched forward and began speeding down the runway.

In less than half the length of the runway the plane leapt into the air and they were airborne. Marsha had a perfect view of the emerald green jungle canopy below as Buck banked the plane into a turn heading east for Kisangani.

"So, you're a paleontologist like Bruce?" Buck asked trying to make small talk.

"Yeah, Bruce and I went to college together back in the day," she told him.

"Well, maybe between the two of you you'll be able to capture one of those Mokele-mbembe monsters," he replied.

"Don't tell me that you believe in this river monster too?" she asked.

"Hell yes I believe it's real because I've see the thing a couple of times flying over the river," he told her.

"You actually saw an animal in the river that looked like a plesiosaur?" she asked.

"Well, I don't know what that is, but I think that's what I saw. Of course Bruce told me it was probably just an old tree floating in the river," he replied.

Marsha remained silent. Just as she had thought, Buck was just another one of those people that perpetuate a myth without any real firsthand knowledge. She knew the same thing had happened in Tibet with the Yeti. Lots of people purportedly saw the creature or say they were even attacked by it, but none of them had any real evidence that it existed.

Marsha's silence didn't deter Buck from continuing to talk about the Mokele-mbembe. "I guess almost every tribesman along the river has seen the monster at one time or another. They say that sometimes it snatches young children right off the river bank and eats them," he told her.

Marsha's reaction to that bit of news was to immediately think it was large crocodiles that were killing the children, but she said, "Well, I hope we can catch one."

"The natives say it's about twenty feet long, so you're going to need a lot of heavy equipment and nets, not to mention an army of natives to help you," Buck suggested.

"Well, we've got to find one first before we can begin to think about capturing it," Marsha replied.

"Oh, I don't think you'll have much trouble finding one of the creatures, the natives see them quite often," Buck replied.

Buck sat up in his seat as if something had shocked him. "Hey, I just had a great idea," he said. "Why don't you get yourself one of those tranquilizer dart guns they use for putting elephants to sleep when they want to check them for whatever?" he suggested. "If one of those dart things can put an elephant to sleep, they ought to be able to put Mokele-mbembe to sleep too."

"That is a good idea. I'll see if Bruce can get us one of those tranquilizer dart guns," she replied.

During the remainder of the flight both Buck and Marsha remained silent. Marsha was truly amazed at the density of the emerald green jungle canopy below. After living in the Gobi desert for so long, it was a joy to see so many trees.

She was also surprised at the number of large rivers they crossed as they traveled east toward Kisangani. She guessed they were the tributaries of the Congo that Bruce had mentioned.

"How much longer is it to Kisangani," Marsha asked.

"We should be able to see it pretty soon," Buck told her.

He was right. About fifteen minutes later Marsha saw a single runway carved out of the jungle. The runway was paved, and had some buildings off to one side.

Buck circled the field as he requested landing instructions from the tower. Marsha assumed that was merely a formality because there was no other traffic over the field, and there was only the single runway to land on.

He brought the plane down in a very smooth landing and then taxied over to the group of buildings, one of which was the passenger terminal. As soon as the propellers stopped turning they all exited the plane. Buck took their luggage out of the plane, set it on the ground and said, "Well, I wish you guys luck on finding Mokele-mbembe. I wish I was going with you, but I've got a few more charters coming up soon, so I got to keep flying."

Bruce and Marsha carried their luggage to the front of the terminal and looked round for a taxi. A few minutes later a taxi pulled up to the curb in front of them. As the driver was putting their luggage in the trunk Bruce told him they were going to the Hotel Royal. Marsha didn't say anything, but she hoped the hotel at least had hot and cold running water.

On the drive to the hotel Marsha was surprised at the devastation she saw on almost every city block. There were many houses and buildings that were just burnt out hulks of what they originally were. There were also burned cars on every street. Bruce saw the surprise on Marsha's face. "I know it looks bad, but remember, they had a terrible war here not too long ago and it will take them many years to get everything back to normal," he told her.

"Yes, I vaguely remember hearing about it on the news. It was the Hutu tribe against the Tutsi tribe wasn't it?" she asked.

"Yeah, them and a few other tribes and countries all fighting and massacring each other. It was a really bloody few years and pretty much tore the country apart," Bruce told her.

"Is it safe now?" she asked, somewhat concerned about their safety.

"Oh it's safe enough now. I guess all parties got tired of killing each other so they made a truce a couple years ago," Bruce replied.

As they neared the hotel the streets got worse with more burned out buildings and cars. But when the hotel came into sight Marsha was surprised. It was a modern hotel that looked very clean and inviting.

"Let's check in and put our luggage in our rooms and then I'll take you to see my evidence," Bruce suggested.

"Okay, I'm dying to see why you brought me half way around the world," Marsha replied laughing.

They checked into the hotel, put their bags in their rooms, and were in front of the hotel ready to go in less than fifteen minutes. Bruce hailed a taxi and told the driver to take them to the ice house down by the river.

On the ride to the ice house Marsha tried to get Bruce to tell her what they were going to see, but he was adamant that she had to wait to see it in person. Finally the taxi pulled up in front of a corrugated steel building. "Here is the ice house Bwana," the driver announced proudly.

Bruce paid the driver and they got out and went inside the building. A short very black man greeted them, "Hello, I am so happy to see you again Bwana Bruce."

"It is good to see you again also Mguala," Bruce replied. "Do you still have my large friend here?" he asked.

"Yes, Bwana, he is still here, but I hope you will get him out of here soon," Mguala said.

Mguala led them to a door and opened it. They went inside and Marsha saw something large on the floor covered with green canvas, with shaved ice covering it. Bruce reached down and took hold of the canvas and in one motion threw aside the ice and the canvas.

To Marsha's surprise beneath the canvas was a large crocodile in two pieces. "What the hell is this Bruce?" she asked, somewhat irritated.

"Calm down Marsha. This large crocodile was bitten in half with one single bite, and I believe it was by Mokelembembe," he told her.

"Come on Bruce, any other large crocodile could have bitten this guy in two," Marsha replied.

"Of course you're right, except for one thing. This crocodile has twelve vertebrae missing. That means the mouth that bit this monster in half was at least a foot and half wide, maybe even two feet wide, and no crocodile has a mouth that wide," he explained.

"Are you sure about the vertebrae?" she asked.

"Yes, but that's not all. Some natives told me that there was a woman washing clothes in the river and that this crocodile was swimming towards her. Some people on the shore began shouting at her to get out of the water, when suddenly they saw Mokele-mbembe's head come out of the water and bite this one in half," Bruyce told her.

"And you believe them?" she asked.

"They have no reason to lie about a thing like that. Besides, I'm telling you that natives all up and down the river, and even in many of the tributaries claim to have seen Mokele-mbembe," Bruce replied. "I think you need to talk to some of them and see how sincere they are," he added.

"I think the correct word is 'superstitious' not 'sincere,' Marsha replied sarcastically.

"Does that mean you're not going to join me in an expedition to try to get one of these monsters?" he asked.

"Well, I'm already here in Africa so it would be kind of stupid for me not to follow through with you on your crazy goose chase," she replied laughing.

"Great! I knew I could count on you. I'll get us some porters and all the supplies we'll need, plus some dugouts. We can be ready in a week, meanwhile we can enjoy the amenities of beautiful Kisangani," he said jokingly.

"Do you know anybody that might have a tranquilizer gun for elephants?" she asked.

"No, but it should be easy enough to find someone. I think someone in the national park service probably has one. I'll check and see," he replied.

Mguala, who had been standing to one side listening to Bruce and Marsha talking, asked, "Bwana, can I get rid of the crocodile now that the Memsaab has seen it?"

"Yes Mguala, you can do whatever you want with him now," Bruce replied. He pulled a wad of Congolese francs from his pocket and handed it to the native, "Here's a little tip for keeping it such a long time for me."

They returned to the hotel where Bruce immediately busied himself preparing for their expedition, and Marsha went to her room to get a bath and change of clothes. After more than eight phone calls Bruce finally got in touch with a man named Pierre Melot who was the man in charge of the park rangers in the Odzala National Park.

When Bruce told him that he wanted use of a tranquilizer dart gun powerful enough to bring down an elephant, Melot assured him that he had several such guns. However, when Bruce told him why he wanted the gun, Melot fell silent. A few seconds later he asked, "You're kidding right?"

32

"No, I am absolutely serious. Dr. Marsha Styles and I are mounting an expedition to either kill or capture one of the Mokele-mbembe," Bruce told him.

"You know of course that the monster is only a legend don't you?" Melot asked.

"I know that every white man believes it is only a legend, but I have fairly good proof that some large animal lives in the rivers here," Bruce explained.

Again Melot remained silent for several second. "Can I join you on this hair brained expedition of yours?" he asked.

Bruce was completely surprised and a little suspicious, "You mean you want to join us on the expedition?" he asked.

"Yes, if you'll have me. I have lots of experience in the bush, I'm easy to get along with, and most importantly I have the gun you want," he replied.

"How come you went from 'hair brained' expedition, to wanting to come with us? Bruce asked.

Melot remained silent for a long time before answering. "The truth is I think maybe I saw the creature about four years ago. It was only for a second, but I swear I saw what looked like a large fin rise up out of the river and then disappear again beneath the water."

"And you've remained silent about seeing it for all these years?" Bruce asked.

"Well, you know, it's sort of like seeing a flying saucer. If you do see one you don't want to tell anybody about it because they'll think you're crazy. So yes, I've kept it a secret all these years," Melot told him.

"Well, you're more than welcome to come with us. We're staying in the Royal Hotel here in Kisangani, and it'll probably take me a week to put the expedition together," Bruce explained.

"Okay, I'll be there in about four days. I have a few loose ends to take care of here in the Odzala first, and then fly to Kinsangani," Melot said.

"Don't forget to bring your tranquilizer gun and lots of darts," Bruce reminded him.

When he finished talking to Melot, Bruce put out the word that he was looking for eight natives to work as porters on an expedition to hunt down Mokele-mbembe. In this country where jobs were impossible to find, he expected to have several hundred eager applicants within a few days.

The only thing left to do to prepare for the expedition was to purchase the supplies they would need, and to rent several dugouts. He figured he could wait until tomorrow to get started on that.

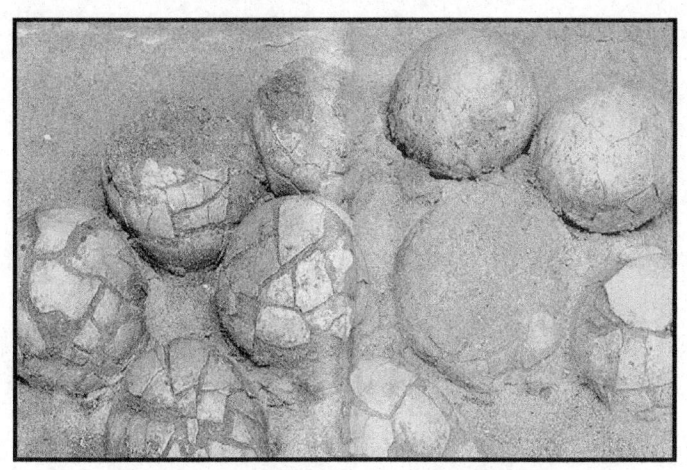

Gobi Desert Dinosaur Eggs

Airport at Chengdu, China

Sandwich Shop at Nairobi Airport

Congo River

Village on Congo River

Congo River

Large Gar type fish in Congo River

Photograph of suspected Mokele-mbembe

Artist's rendering of Mokele-mbembe

And some say there are no monsters in Africa

CHAPTER THREE

Bruce was surprised at the response to his request for porters for the expedition. He had hundreds of men to show up for the job, but he found that they were staying away in droves! It seemed that the natives wanted no part of an expedition to hunt Mokele-mbembe.

When Pierre arrived four days later he suggested that Bruce offer to pay twice the going rate for porters. Even in the Congo money talks. Bruce did that and within the following three days he had signed up five men for the expedition.

The first one to sign on to the expedition was Fabrice, a forty-five year old man from the Luba tribe, He spoke several tribal languages, as well as French and English, so Bruce made him the lead porter.

The second man to sign up to be a porter for the expedition was named Tresor. He was twenty years old and a member of the Kongo tribe. Tresor was almost six feet tall and looked very strong, a trait always welcomed in a porter because they often had to carry heavy loads.

The next porter to join the expedition was named Blaise. He was only seventeen, but he looked strong and seemed intelligent. Perhaps his best quality was that he was enthusiastic about trying to catch Mokele-mbembe. Like Tresor, Blaise was from the Kongo tribe.

Bruce was about to give up on getting any more porters when a young man named Arsene came to apply for the job. He was thirty-two years old, and according to him, was a very good cook. He told Bruce that he had worked in a hotel restaurant until the war came and rebel soldiers burned the hotel because the owner was French. "I can cook fancy French dishes if Bwana wants," he told Bruce.

The last porter to join the expedition was named Yannick. He from the Luba tribe, about forty years old (he wasn't sure of his age), and had been a fisherman on the river for many years. According to him he had seen the Mokele-mbembe once about eleven years ago and would love to be in on either killing or catching one.

While Bruce was lining up the porters and arranging for the supplies they would need Marsha began organizing her notes and photos for her book about the Gobi desert expedition hunting fossilized dinosaur nests and eggs. Every evening at dinner Bruce would bring her up to date on how preparations for the expedition were going. They also went to the hotel bar every night after dinner and had a few drinks. Pierre was usually there too and it gave them a chance to get to know him a little before they began the expedition.

Pierre turned out to be an interesting fellow. Before coming to the Congo and becoming a park ranger, he had been a captain in the French Foreign Legion, and had fought in both Algeria and Mali. He had a great love for animals and became a park ranger to help stop the massive poaching of wild animals by the Congolese natives. 'Bush meat,' as the natives called it was an important part of their diet, but it was devastating to the animal population of the country.

At last the day arrived for them to begin the expedition. Bruce had hired four good sized dugouts for an exorbitant price. He had the porters load all the supplies into them and they were ready to shove off. Bruce had Fabrice and Marsha together in one dugout, Tresor and Pierre in another, Arsene and Blaise in one, and he and Yannick together in one.

His plan was to begin going down river slowly, stopping at any villages along the banks and inquiring if anybody had seen a Mokele-mbembe or any other unusual large animal in the river lately. Bruce knew they were searching for a needle in a haystack, but he could think of no other way to try to find one. There was also the off chance they might see one as they paddled down river.

The first day they traveled approximately twenty kilometers without coming across any villages along the bank. They could have passed over a hundred Mokele-mbembes without knowing it because the water was so muddy and deep. Bruce knew that the Congo River was the deepest river in the world, with many areas where it was two hundred feet deep. In short, it was the perfect place for a large aquatic animal to live without ever being seen.

Just before dusk they beached their dugouts and made camp for the night. The porters set up their tents and Arsene built a fire and began preparing their dinner. Two hours later, to the surprise of Bruce, Marsha, and Pierre, they were served a delicious ragout for dinner.

The other porters had built their own cooking fire and prepared their own food separate from the bwanas. It smelled like meat cooking so Bruce assumed they had brought some bush meat with them. It was probably a small antelope or maybe even a monkey. Whatever it was it smelled pretty good to Bruce.

When they finished eating Bruce, Marsha and Pierre went down to the river and sat on the bank to discuss the expedition in general and what they were going to do tomorrow specifically. Pierre pulled his pipe from his pants pocket and filled it with tobacco and tamped it down with his finger. Then he struck a match and lit it. He had just exhaled a large puff of smoke when suddenly there was a loud splash in the river right in front of them.

Unfortunately it was too dark to see anything, but they all had the same thought. Was it the Mokele-mbembe that made the splash? Of course that was wishful thinking because there were dozens of species of large fish that could have made the splash. None of them said a word about what they were thinking.

The following morning after breakfast the porters loaded everything back into the dugouts and they continued their way down river. After traveling just a few kilometers they came across a small village on the right bank of the river. It consisted of only twelve small houses, and perhaps forty people including the children.

Nobody in the village had seen or knew anything about the Mokele-mbembe, but Bruce did manage to buy two very large catfish from them. Each fish was about four feet long and weighed at least fifty pounds, so they would provide the entire expedition with a nice evening meal of fried catfish.

They continued down river paddling slowly hoping to see some indication of Mokele-mbembe. They were looking for a hump of the animal's back to rise up out of the murky river water, or perhaps a large fin as Pierre said he had seen so many years ago, or maybe a large head emerge from the water. But they saw nothing unusual, absolutely nothing at all.

They pulled their dugouts up to the bank again at dusk to make camp. Just as the night before, the porters unloaded the dugouts and set up the tents while Arsene started his cooking fire. While waiting for the fire to catch hold he began to cut up the catfish in portion sized pieces, which he placed on the grill. Then he wrapped some sweet potatoes in large green leaves and placed them on the grill also.

Soon the rich smell of grilled catfish and sweet potatoes permeated the camp area. Marsha came over to where Bruce and Pierre were talking and said, "Bruce, I think you picked a winner for our camp cook."

"Yeah, I know, he really seems to know what he is doing," Bruce replied.

"Tomorrow I think I'll kill an antelope so we can have some steaks for dinner. I like fish well enough, but I'm really more of a red meat man," Pierre said.

"I'm with you, I would die for a good steak," Marsha said laughing.

At last Arsene announced that dinner was ready. They all had to admit that the grilled catfish was a real treat, and the sweet potatoes were delicious! After dinner Bruce, Pierre, and Marsha sat around the fire smoking and talking. Pierre took a real interest in Marsha's work in China searching for fossilized dinosaur nests and eggs. He was especially impressed that she had found areas where there were dozens of nests all in one area. "Most people don't think of dinosaurs as being social animals, but from what you found it sounds to me like they were," Pierre said.

"Yes, as a matter of fact we were quite surprised to find out how social they seemed to be," Marsha replied. "Of course there is still lots of research to be done, but my theory is that the smaller dinosaurs stayed together in herds or packs to protect themselves from larger predators, much the way many small species of fish group together in large schools as a protective measure.

"It sounds reasonable to me. I know that gnus herd together as protection from lions and cheetas," Pierre said.

Marsha laughed. "Yeah, but the ones at the edge of the herd still get eaten," she said.

The following morning after breakfast the porters were packing all their gear into the dugouts when a dugout approached from downriver. As soon as it was close enough one of the natives in the dugout shouted, "Is there a doctor with your party?"

Bruce shouted back, "No, but what is the problem, why do you need a doctor? Maybe we can help in some way."

"No, we need a doctor. A woman just had half her leg bitten off by a Mokele-mbembe," the man said excitedly.

"Are you sure it was a Mokele-mbembe that bit her?" Bruce asked.

"Yes Bwana, the lady was standing knee deep in the river washing some pots when the monster raised its head up out of the water and then dived down and bit the lady's leg off. I saw it with my own eyes Bwana," the man said.

"How far away is this lady?" Marsha asked.

"Not far Memsaab, maybe one half hour if we paddle fast," one of the natives replied. "But we must hurry before she bleeds too much," he added.

"Did you bandage her leg?" Marsha asked.

"Yes Memsaab, we wrapped lots of rags around her leg and tied them on with rope, but she needs a doctor to bandage her properly," he replied.

"Come on Bruce, let's you and I go now and Pierre and the others can follow as soon as they are ready," Marsha urged, as she grabbed their first aid kit and put it in the bottom of their boat.

They got into their dugout and followed the natives downriver to where the injured woman was. It didn't take long, and when they got there they pulled their dugout up onto the bank. Marsha grabbed their first aid kit and they followed the two natives to the bamboo hut where they had taken the woman.

It took a few minutes for their eyes to adjust to the dim light inside the hut. Finally they could see a woman laying on some blankets on the floor. She looked to be about twenty-five years old, and bottom half of her left leg was missing. Just as the native had said, the stub was wrapped in old rags tied on with a small rope. Luckily, the rope had acted as a tourniquet and had nearly stopped the bleeding completely.

Marsha checked if the woman was in shock. She didn't show any signs of it so Marsha untied the rope and removed the rags from her leg. She washed the bloody stump with alcohol to disinfect it and then bandaged it again with large gauze bandages and taped it all in place. It was obvious that the woman was in considerable pain so she gave her a shot of morphine before leaving.

As she was exiting the hut the other two dugouts pulled up onto the bank. "So, is there any truth to what that guy said about Mokele-mbembe attacking a woman?" Pierre shouted.

"Well, something took off her leg all right, but we haven't had time to talk to any of the witnesses so far," Marsha replied.

There was a small crowd of natives gathered to find out of the woman was going to live, so Pierre shouted, "Did any of you see the animal that bit the woman's leg?"

Three men and one woman stepped forward, all of them saying that they saw the Mokele-mbembe attack the woman.

"Can you show us the exact spot where the woman was standing when she was attacked?" Bruce asked.

They led them to the edge of the river and pointed to a spot about six feet out from the bank. "She was standing right there washing a pot when the monster came and bit her leg," said the woman.

"Did any of you see which way the monster went after biting the woman?" Bruce asked.

"I saw the hump of the beast's back going downriver. It wasn't swimming, just sort of floating along with the current, so maybe you could catch it if you hurry," one of the men said.

It didn't seem very likely that they could actually catch up with whatever had attacked the woman, but it was worth a try anyway. After all, that was what they were there for, and it was the best lead they had so far.

Within ten minutes they were all in their dugouts heading downriver paddling as fast as they could. As they were speeding along it occurred to Marsha that they could very well be passing right over the top of the animal they were after. After all the water was muddy and deep enough that they could pass over the top of a whale and not know it.

After travelling downriver for nearly three hours one of the natives in the lead dugout started pointing ahead and shouted, "I see it. There it is! It's the Mokele-mbembe alright!"

Bruce stood up in the dugout and looked where the native was pointing. Suddenly he saw it about fifty yards up ahead. It appeared to be the slightly curved back of a large aquatic animal. The part of its back that was up out of the water looked to be about five or six feet long.

As they drew closer to the animal it became apparent that it was completely unaware of their presence. Bruce had made the right decision when he decided to use native dugouts rather than more modern boats with motors.

Bruce picked up one of the harpoons he had laying in the bottom of the dugout and attached a long rope to it. He stood up in the bow of the dugout and waited until they were only a couple feet away from the animal, and then he thrust the harpoon into it with all his might.

The beast's reaction was immediate and violent. It raised its head up out of the water and turned it backwards trying to bite at whatever it was that was causing it so much pain. The movement was so fast that Bruce only got a quick glance of the animal's head, and it looked like it might be some sort of plesiosaur species. One thing was certain, it had lots of teeth in that big mouth!

After snapping wildly at whatever was causing it pain, it dove under water and sped away. The rope attached to the harpoon went singing out of the dugout as the animal went deeper and deeper beneath the murky water. Finally it slowed down enough for Bruce and the porters in the dugout to grab the rope and begin pulling the beast to the top again.

Bruce yelled, "Pierre, if we can get this thing up to the surface, I want you to shoot it with your tranquilizer gun!"

"Okay, I'll be ready," Pierre replied, and began loading a tranquilizer dart into the rifle.

It took over half an hour to get the big animal to the surface. Bruce lost track of how many times they had it close to the surface when suddenly it would dive towards the bottom again. The men were not strong enough to keep it from diving whenever it wanted to.

They finally managed to get it to the surface long enough for Pierre to get a shot at it. The tranquilizer dart hit it in the back and stuck. As expected, the dart caused the animal to dive beneath the muddy waters of the river headed for the bottom.

Within twenty minutes the tranquilizer took effect and the animal was just dead weight on the end of the rope. They paddled their dugouts over to the bank and got out. Standing on the bank they began to pull the animal up to the surface. Tensions were high as everybody waited to see the Mokele-mbembe for the first time.

CHAPTER FOUR

The first part of the animal to clear the murky water was its head. It had a long thin mouth full of very sharp teeth, and looked like it could be related somehow to a plesiosaur. But then came its long body revealing rather large pectoral fins. It was obviously some sort of very large fish!

Pierre was the first to recognize it as a gigantic gar. It was nearly sixteen feet long, and probably weighed about fifteen hundred pounds. It was a wonderful monster-sized fish, but it wasn't a Mokele-mbembe, and may or may not be the animal that bit the woman's leg off. The porters pulled the animal up onto the bank and Marsha took photographs of it. It was the biggest gar fish that any of them had ever seen.

The question of whether or not this was the animal that had bitten off the leg of the woman was soon solved. One of the porters cut the beast open and found the lower part of her leg in its stomach.

As soon as she saw the leg Marsha turned away from the scene. There was something about seeing a human leg come from inside the stomach of such an animal that made her feel nauseous.

Once they got over the disappointment of the animal not being the Mokele-mbembe they decided to camp for the night right there where they were. There was still lots of daylight left so Pierre and one of the porters went off in the bush to hunt for some meat for their evening meal.

They returned two hours later carrying a small antelope known as a reedbuck. Arsene quickly set to work skinning and butchering the animal in preparation for their evening meal. Although it was small, it would provide more than enough meat for everyone in their party, with enough left over for breakfast in the morning.

For the next three weeks they continued paddling downstream looking for any sign of a large aquatic animal. At every riverside village they stopped to ask the inhabitants if they had seen the Mokele-mbembe. None of the people they talked to had seen the animal, but they were all sure that it was real. They had all heard stories of people or livestock being eaten by the beast, and they believed them to be true.

Marsha had long since grown bored with their search for Mokele-mbembe and now devoted nearly all her time to working on her book on her laptop. If nothing else was accomplished on this expedition, she was going to get a lot done on her book about the Chinese expedition.

Just when it seemed like this Mokele-mbembe was too illusive to get a look at much less kill or capture it, their luck changed. They came upon a village where the natives excitedly told them that a Mokele-mbembe had been lurking in the waters adjacent to their village for over a week. It had killed and eaten four villagers so far, and they were now afraid to go anywhere near the riverbank.

"Have you actually seen the Mokele-mbembe?" Bruce asked the village elders.

"Oh yes, bwana, the beast is very large indeed and has a big mouth with lots of teeth. It lurks beneath the murky waters and when someone gets into the water or is even stranding close to the river on the bank it raises its head and attacks," the oldest of the elders replied.

"Are you sure it's not a crocodile?" Bruce asked.

"Oh no, bwana, this animal is much larger indeed than a crocodile. For sure bwana, it is a Mokele-mbembe!" the old man insisted.

Bruce was well aware that the natives were inclined to exaggeration. But there was something about the terror he saw in the old man's eyes that convinced him that there was something different and terrifying lurking in the deep dark waters adjacent to the village.

Bruce and Pierre decided to try to either kill or catch whatever it was that was terrifying the natives of this village. Their plan was for Pierre to kill a small antelope that they could use as bait to draw the monster to the top of the water.

They unloaded all their gear from the dugouts and set up camp near the village. While the porters were setting up camp, Pierre and one of the porters went off into the bush to hunt an antelope. While Pierre was gone, Bruce and Marsha laid out all the equipment they might possibly need to catch whatever monster was in the river.

Bruce had purchased some old cargo nets and had them all tied together into one large, very strong net. He also bought several large fish hooks of the size and type used by professional shark fishermen, hundreds of feet of both rope and small steel cable, and had a blacksmith in Kisangani make six large harpoons for him. And of course Bruce had a large caliber rifle of the type used for hunting elephants. Also Pierre had both a large caliber hunting rifle and two tranquilizer guns.

As Bruce surveyed the equipment, he felt satisfied that they had everything they would need to catch whatever monster was there. And if for some reason they couldn't capture it, he was certain they could kill it.

Pierre was gone for over four hours, but when he returned he and the porter were carrying a fairly large antelope. They had it trussed up by its legs on a long pole, and each of them was carrying an end of the pole on his shoulders.

It was almost dusk so they decided to wait until the next morning to set their trap for the monster. That night, after dinner, they sat around the fire talking about how they were going to go about trying to capture the animal.

Bruce said, "Okay, first thing in the morning we will stake out the dead antelope about five or six feet out into the river. That way if the animal comes to grab it, we will be close enough on the bank to either harpoon it, or shoot it with the tranquilizer gun."

"Don't you think we should put some of the porters in the dugouts out on the river ready with the cargo nets to throw over the beast?" Pierre asked.

"If this animal, whatever it is, is as large and dangerous as the villagers say it is, I think it would be foolish to put any of our porters in a position where they might fall into the water and get attacked or killed," Marsh replied.

"I agree with Marsha," Bruce said, "if the monster does come to take our bait and we shoot it with the tranquilizer gun or harpoon it, the animal is not going to just lay there. It is going to be thrashing around and everything is going to be extremely chaotic for quite a while, and any dugout nearby would probably tip over and throw its occupants into the river."

"Yes, we'll have to keep everybody well away from the edge of the river, because when the monster take the bait all hell is going to break loose and we don't want any innocent bystanders to get hurt," Marsha said.

They continued talking about their plan to capture the animal well into the night. By the time they turned in all three of them felt confident they had thought of everything possible to ensure a successful 'monster' hunt in the morning.

Marsha awoke before Bruce and Pierre, and Arsene already had the cook fire going and the coffee pot boiling. "Would Memsaab like some coffee?" he asked.

"Some coffee would be wonderful Arsene," she replied.

The cook poured a cup of coffee and handed it to her. It smelled wonderful! "Thank you Arsene," she said.

She took a sip and sat down to enjoy it. No sooner had she sat down when Bruce came out of his tent rubbing his eyes to get the sleep out of them. He looked at Marsha and said, "Good morning. Well, are you ready to capture a Mokele-mbembe?"

"I'll be ready as soon as I finish this coffee and have a little breakfast," she replied smiling.

"Yeah, I think I need some of that coffee too," he replied. "Have you seen Pierre this morning?" he asked.

"No, I guess he's still asleep. Why don't you go wake him up so we can get this show on the road?" she suggested.

Just then Pierre came out of his tent. "Good morning everybody," he said cheerfully. "All set to capture the elusive beast of the Congo River this morning?" he asked.

"Just as soon as we have some breakfast," Marsha replied.

Arsene announced that breakfast was ready and each of them grabbed a plate and the cook served them bacon and eggs, and a roll. As were all his meals this breakfast was delicious.

When they finished eating Pierre lit a cigarette, and Marsha and Bruce got another cup of coffee. Not all of the porters had finished eating yet so they had to wait on them. One of the first porters to finish eating was Fabrice. He came over to Bruce to talk to him.

"Bwana, we were talking to some of the villagers last night and none of us wants to go on the river in the dugouts to try to get this animal. They told us that a week ago it tipped over a dugout with three men in it and one of them was never seen again," he said.

"Don't worry Fabrice, we have already decided that it is too dangerous to have anybody on the river while we capture this beast," Bruce assured him. Fabrice went back and told the other porters that they didn't have to go on the river.

After he told them that they all looked over at Bruce. He nodded to them, indicating that what Fabrice told them was true, and they all smiled widely.

"Okay everybody, let's get going, we've got a monster to catch," Bruce said.

They tied a long rope to the dead antelope and two porters threw it out into the river as far as they could. Ideally they would anchor the animal to the river bottom so it wouldn't float away with the current, but the bottom was too deep in that area. As the current caught hold of the antelope it started floating downstream but the rope pulled it over to the riverbank about one hundred feet down river.

They tied the end of the rope to a tree and went down to where the bait was bobbing up and down in the current. Bruce, Marsha, and two of their porters were carrying harpoons. Pierre had his large tranquilizer gun. They felt they were ready if the beast showed itself.

For the next two hours they all waited on the bank, eyes fixed on the antelope carcass bobbing up and down in the river. Pierre was smoking one cigarette after another while Bruce and Marsha spent their time talking and drinking cup after cup of black coffee.

Suddenly the antelope carcass went completely under water and a few seconds later an enormous head rose up out of the river with the antelope in its mouth. It looked like a crocodile but the head alone was easily five feet long. Then, just as suddenly as it had appeared, the monster disappeared beneath the murky water, leaving only a swirling eddy of turbulent water. Everyone was so startled by what they saw that they just stood there holding their weapons.

"Holy Crap!" Pierre exclaimed. "Did you see the size of that thing?"

"There's no way we're ever going to capture that monster. I didn't know crocodiles could get that big, and if I hadn't seen it with my own eyes I wouldn't believe it," Marsha exclaimed.

Bruce said, "I think we just saw the closest thing to a dinosaur we're ever going to see. Pierre, we're going to need another antelope!"

"I think we're going to need several antelopes to get that monster!" Pierre replied.

Since their monster hunting that day was over they all retired to camp to rethink their tactics for killing the monster crocodile. They all knew they would need more than harpoons and tranquilizer guns.

Back in the village as they were trying to figure out a way to kill the crocodile Marsha came up with a plan they all agreed might work. They would get the village blacksmith to forge a very large four-pronged grappling hook for them. Then they would cut open the stomach of the bait antelope and insert the hook inside the animal and then sew it back up. A long thin steel cable would be attached to the grappling hook and tied to a large tree.

When the giant crocodile bites down on the bait the giant hook will embed itself deep in the croc's soft mouth, and he will be unable to shake it out. Then by pulling on the cable they can pull the animal up to the bank where they can get at it with their rifles and harpoons.

Pierre and two of their porters and three villagers went into the bush to hunt for antelope. Just before nightfall they returned with three good sized animals. Their cook, Arsene, took one of them to butcher for the evening meal, and the other two were used as bait animals. Now that they knew they were up against a gigantic crocodile and not some type of throwback dinosaur, they were certain they would be able to kill it the following morning.

The villagers were jubilant knowing that the beast that had been killing them would be eliminated in the morning. That evening they organized several dances to ensure the death of the crocodile, and also to celebrate the white hunters that were going to kill it.

The villagers' dancing and singing lasted long into the night, until the last fire burned down to a pile of glowing embers. As Marsha, Bruce, and Pierre drifted off to sleep they could still hear the drums in the village beating out dance rhythms.

The following morning everybody was up early, and after breakfast and coffee were ready to take on the monster sized crocodile. As they prepared to toss the first bait carcass into the river, nearly all the villagers came down to the river bank to watch their nemesis defeated.

Four porters tossed the carcass as far out into the river as they could. The cable was already tied to a large tree. As the carcass slowly worked its way back to the riverbank everybody anxiously awaited the crocodile's attack.

They didn't have long to wait. Within an hour of throwing the bait carcass into the river the monster crocodile raised its head up out of the water, opened its gigantic mouth and swallowed the antelope in one bite. As it started to swim away the barbs on the grappling hook embedded themselves deep into the crocodile's innards.

The pain caused the beast to come to the surface and roll over and over as it tried to dislodge the hooks from inside its belly. All the rolling and thrashing about only caused the hooks to sink themselves deeper into the animal's innards.

It continued to try to dislodge the hooks for over an hour, until it wore itself out thrashing about. Seeing that the animal was now resting on the surface of the river,

Bruce shouted, "Come on everybody, let's grab the cable and pull this beast up onto the bank."

Over twenty men and boys grabbed onto the cable and began pulling the beast closer to the riverbank. As it neared the bank it suddenly charged forward and pulled itself up onto the bank, its massive jaws trying to bite anything it could reach. Everybody that had been pulling on the cable dropped it immediately and ran for their life.

Luckily everyone managed to escape the beast's jaws. The cable tethering the beast to the tree was only one hundred feet long so the animal could go no further than that.

When the animal reached the end of the cable it stopped, and looked at the large group of people just out of its reach. That's when Pierre shot it with his tranquilizer gun. The dart stuck into the crocodile's side but the beast showed no sign of feeling it. Pierre reloaded the gun and fired another dart into the croc's side, and again there was no reaction from the animal.

"Those darts ought to put the bastard to sleep in about twenty minutes," Pierre said to nobody in particular.

"Well, if it doesn't go to sleep soon I'll shoot the thing in the head with my elephant gun," Bruce told him.

Everybody present waited patiently for the tranquilizer drug to have an effect on the great beast. At last the animal closed its eyes and was obviously in a deep drug induced stupor. One of the braver village warriors jumped on top of the beast and sunk his long spear deep into the animal's head.

Whether it was skill or luck, the warrior had sunk his spear into the crocodile's small brain. Its body twitched two or three times and then went limp. The villagers let out a loud cheer when they realized that the beast that had been menacing them for over a month was dead.

A good many of the villagers stood beside the beast and insisted that Marsha take a picture of them. After taking the picture as requested with her digital camera, Marsha downloaded the photograph into her laptop so the villagers could see it there.

Bruce and Pierre measured the beast and found that it measured twenty-seven feet four inches from the tip of its nose to the end of its tail. "This has to be the biggest crocodile ever killed," Bruce said.

"I'm sure it is. I have never heard of any this size before. This thing must be over sixty years old," Pierre replied.

That evening the village held a feast in honor of the three white hunters. There was tons of native food and drink, and the natives put on a series of dances and songs for their honored guests.

As they were seated cross-legged on the ground enjoying the food and festivities, Marsha asked Bruce if they were going to continue looking for Mokele-mbembe.

"No, although I still believe that the Mokele-mbembe may exist, I don't think we will ever find one. The river is too good at hiding its inhabitants, no matter how big they are," he replied.

THE END

Printed in Great Britain
by Amazon

65951012R00041